+ AN

THE L   ANT

SLEEP +

S

EP

CARL-JOHAN FORSSÉN EHRLIN
ILLUSTRATED BY SYDNEY HANSON

ALSO BY CARL-JOHAN FORSSÉN EHRLIN

THE RABBIT WHO WANTS TO FALL ASLEEP

ACKNOWLEDGEMENTS

THANK YOU TO ALL THE TEST PILOTS WHO READ THE MANUSCRIPT TO THEIR CHILDREN AND GAVE ME VALUABLE FEEDBACK! MY EARLY READERS EVA HYLLSTAM, FREDRIK PRAESTO AND ELIN WESTERBERG; JULIA ANGELIN AND HER COLLEAGUES AT THE SALOMONSSON AGENCY; AND, ABOVE ALL, MY WONDERFUL AND SUPPORTIVE WIFE, LINDA EHRLIN, WHO HAS CONTRIBUTED SO MANY WISE THOUGHTS.

LADYBIRD BOOKS

UK | USA | Canada | Ireland | Australia
India | New Zealand | South Africa

Ladybird Books is part of the Penguin Random House group of companies
whose addresses can be found at global.penguinrandomhouse.com.

www.penguin.co.uk   www.puffin.co.uk   www.ladybird.co.uk

Originally published in Sweden as *Elefanten som så gärna ville somna* copyright © 2016
by Carl-Johan Forssén Ehrlin. Published by agreement with the Salomonsson Agency.

001

Text and illustrations copyright © Carl-Johan Forssén Ehrlin and Ehrlin Publishing AB, 2016
English translation copyright © Neil Smith, 2016
Illustrations by Sydney Hanson

The moral right of the author and illustrator has been asserted

Printed and bound in Italy

A CIP catalogue record for this book is available from the British Library

Hardback ISBN: 978–0–241–29119–1
Paperback ISBN: 978–0–241–29120–7

INSTRUCTIONS TO THE READER

Warning! Use this book with caution. It may cause drowsiness or an unintended catnap. And never read this book out loud close to someone driving any type of vehicle or engaged in any other activity that requires wakefulness!

The author and the publisher very much hope your little one falls asleep, but make no guarantees and can take no responsibility for the outcome.

This book has been written to have a sleep-promoting effect, and therefore sometimes uses unusual language in order to help the child relax and feel ready to sleep. Sometimes the child may need to hear the book a few times before he or she feels comfortable with the story and happily falls asleep.

To achieve the best results when you read this bedtime story, you should read it through to yourself first so that you are familiar with the text and are more free to engage with the story when you read it to your child. I also recommend that you read through the tips at the end of the book in order to get the most out of this sleep-inducing bedtime story. *The Little Elephant Who Wants to Fall Asleep* is also available as an audiobook. You may enjoy listening to this book together as your child falls asleep. You may even fall asleep too, if you desire to do so.

At certain points in the story, it is recommended that you adjust your tone of voice or yawn. Feel your way forward, and see what works best for your child.

• When the text is marked in **bold**, emphasize these words.
• When the text is marked with *italics*, try saying these words in a more soothing voice.
• Where it says [name], feel free to insert your child's name.
• Where it says [yawn], it would be a good idea to do so.

Good luck, and sleep well!

Carl-Johan Forssén Ehrlin

This story is about an elephant named Ellen. She is the kindest and bravest little elephant in the world, and she wants to be your friend and teach you new things. Ellen the Elephant is starting to feel tired now, and she wants you to go with her as she walks to her bed on the other side of the magical forest, where she is going to sleep soundly all night long.

Ellen the Elephant is the same age as you, [name]. She likes doing the same things as you, playing and having fun, on her own and with her friends. Sometimes, when she's playing, the time goes so fast that it's suddenly time to go to bed. So in a lot of ways you're very alike, and you think the same way, [name]. That means it will be easy to follow Ellen as this story helps her to fall asleep.

"I'm starting to feel tired, and I want to go to bed," Ellen the Elephant says to Mummy Elephant [yawn].

"Of course you can **go to bed now,**" Mummy Elephant replies. "Take your friend who's listening to the story through the magical forest to the place where you sleep, and fall fast asleep together. The magical forest is **really good at making children feel sleepy,** and it's lovely and safe for tired children. I wonder how **soon you're going to choose to fall asleep to the story, now** – or in a little while."

Mummy Elephant reminds Ellen, "There are lots of *sleepy* things around you right now, and you, [name], can choose the ones that will best **help you fall asleep.**"

Ellen the Elephant asks Mummy Elephant, "What do you do to **make yourself feel tired**?"

"I usually let everything be sleepy – the sounds and voices around me, and the things I imagine. The way the pillow my head is resting on helps me fall asleep when I say to myself, **Relax.** *It feels so lovely with the covers tucked up around me. That's when I feel most tired, like* **now** *[yawn]."*

Together, you and Ellen the Elephant set off on your adventure, which will make you really tired now. On the hill, Ellen's mummy waves to you sleepily and says, "Goodnight, sweet child, see you in the morning, when you've slept soundly all night."

Ellen the Elephant says to you, "Come with me, and I'll show you where I usually **fall fast asleep**. It doesn't matter if you will easily **fall asleep, before the story is over.** I get tired very quickly when **I'm about to drift off to sleep** and someone is reading me a story."

Ellen says, "Come with me. Let's go into the magical sleepy forest together. So that **you will feel completely calm and safe,** you're welcome to ride on my back. That will help you to **relax and be lulled naturally to sleep,** [name]. I like falling asleep, either in my bed or in the magical forest, **right now.** *They both work just as well, and I feel tired every time I think about it."* Ellen the Elephant yawns [yawn].

Once inside the forest, Ellen the Elephant says calmly and softly, "The forest is full of kind animals who are my friends. Over there, for instance, is where Snoozy Mole lives with his parents."

Snoozy Mole looks out from his home with his **eyes closed** and says, *"Shhh, it's time to be quiet and listen to the story now. I'm about to fall fast asleep. My parents say that when children* **stay still** *to listen to the story right now, they let everything around them gradually fade away. A lot of the time, children also want to lie down and relax so that they can fall asleep too. Like when you feel it's time to fall asleep, and fall asleep now."*

Snoozy Mole goes on: *"Sometimes I pretend I'm not listening and am doing something else, and on those occasions, I feel even more relaxed and tired."* He settles down and **falls asleep now.**

"Now Snoozy Mole and his family are all sleeping. We're the last ones who'll be **falling asleep soon,** [name], with the help of the magical forest," Ellen the Elephant says, and yawns [yawn].

In the magical forest, the wind blows gently through the trees, whispering, "*Sleep well*," which somehow only makes you feel more and more relaxed.

You reach an old flight of steps. Ellen the Elephant tells you they're called the **Sleepy Stairs** because almost all the children who go down the stairs, **now, get really tired** and *just want to lie down comfortably, when you walk down, down, and down.*

"*The staircase has five steps, and with each step we take down the stairs you,* [name], *will feel more and more calm,*" Ellen says.

Here's the first step.

Five. *"Oh, how lovely," you say to yourself, and you let go of all your thoughts and listen to the story. Aaah . . .*

Four. *A lovely relaxing feeling that is even more restful, as your body and thoughts, calm down now.*

Three. *You're even more relaxed,* [name].

Two. *Sleepy and relaxed. Your eyelids are feeling so heavy now.*

One. *Much more tired than before, which feels nice for Ellen the Elephant and you* [yawn].

Zero. *So tired now, you can just let sleep come,* [name].

When you get to the bottom of the Sleepy Stairs, Ellen the Elephant says in a tired voice, *"Come with me to the peaceful stream. There's something sleepy I want to show you."* You choose to go with Ellen to the stream and to keep listening to the story that is making you tired, even if **all you want to do is fall asleep at any moment, now.**

On the way, you see a leaf that's **just as beautiful as you are,** [name], and *that lets go right now* and comes loose from a branch of an old, sleepy tree.

The leaf starts to float freely through the air and follows the wind and the story as it slowly carries you down and down. The leaf is falling so slowly and beautifully. Slowly down, slowly down. Just like your eyes are closing right now.

The leaf keeps falling down and down until it gets close to the peaceful stream, where all the fish are, now, lying asleep, [name]. "Everything that lands in the stream or on the moss alongside it, falls asleep now, almost instantly," Ellen the Elephant explains sleepily to you.

And it's absolutely true. When the leaf lands gently on the soft moss beside the stream, it lets itself be embraced by tiredness and, just relax now. It yawns itself to sleep and is now carried easily off to dreamland.

"I feel like the leaf," Ellen the Elephant says, feeling very tired and ready to join in and fall asleep now [yawn].

When you reach the sleepy stream, you can hear the peaceful, bubbling sound of the little waterfall, which helps you feel all calm inside yourself, now.

On a rock beside the stream, the kind forest troll, Snoring Sophie, is fast asleep. Sometimes she talks in her sleep, and this evening she's doing it again. In a faint, sleepy voice, she murmurs, *"When you dip your feet in the stream, it makes you feel so relaxed."*

Ellen the Elephant and you look at each other and decide to dip your **almost-falling-asleep** feet in *the peaceful and warm, soothing stream. You do that now.*

As soon as your feet enter the lovely warm water, you feel something start to change in your toes. *They're now full of tiredness and are falling fast asleep.*

Snoring Sophie says softly, *"Notice how the tiredness spreads through your body, [name]. How relaxation moves up into both of your legs.*

"Then on to your stomach and across your back, more and more relaxed. Your breathing is getting calmer and slower, now.

"The lovely relaxation spreads out to your arms and fingers. You just let them rest peacefully in your bed.

"The relaxation gets deeper and deeper inside your head. And all your thoughts just want to go to sleep now, [name].

"A calmness and relaxation spreads right through your whole body and is helping you sleep all night, now that you're getting more and more ready to sleep with the story's help [yawn]."

Fully relaxed, the two of you move slowly and carefully back on to the sleepy path again, the path that leads to Ellen the Elephant's lovely bed. If you're not quite tired enough, now, you can just let yourself drift off to sleep with your eyes closed.

Now that you and Ellen are getting closer and closer to the time to fall asleep, you come to a fork in the path. In front of you are two paths, one leading left and one leading right. In the soft light of the moon, you can see the friendly parrot, Dozing Daniel, sitting on a perch.

He tells you, "If you go left, you'll **soon fall fast asleep.** If you go right, you'll **fall asleep twice as quickly and sleep soundly all night through. Fall asleep twice as quickly and sleep soundly all night through.**"

That's true, you think now.

Ellen the Elephant says to you, "I think we should go right and **fall asleep twice as quickly and deeply now, how comforting.** That path will also help us to fall asleep more and more quickly every evening, [name], and sleep well even without this story. It always works for me."

"That really does sound nice," you say to yourself, and you start to walk *twice as deep into sleep* along the path as you repeat to yourself: "**I fall asleep easily and sleep better every night,** both with and without this story [yawn]."

Tomorrow you will wake up rested and full of energy, but now you can just relax and fall asleep.

You decide to continue along the path that will take you to **sleep. You're much more tired now.** After a little while, when you feel even more relaxed, you meet Roger the Rabbit.

"Hello," Roger the Rabbit says. He looks extremely tired.

"Are you feeling tired as well and want to go to sleep now?" asks Ellen the Elephant.

Roger the Rabbit says that he has just been to see Uncle Yawn, who usually helps him fall asleep, and that Roger is **really tired now.** Uncle Yawn gave him some of the powerful and magical sleeping powder so he can share it with you, to help you fall fast asleep.

"When it is sprinkled all over you, it will create a really lovely and relaxing feeling that will make your whole body so, so tired," Roger the Rabbit says.

Ellen the Elephant takes the bag of magical sleeping powder that helps all children, rabbits and elephants to fall asleep. Using her trunk, she sucks up the magical powder and then blows it all over your body, [name]. *The powder lands softly on you, and you now feel a strong longing to fall asleep. A feeling that gets twice as strong with each breath. And, as you think about how sleepy it's making you feel, it feels like a good idea for you to, fall asleep now.*

With sleepy steps, you walk slowly further down the path. Then Muddled Mouse comes walking along, holding her pillow in her paw. "Try to understand what she's saying, and go along with it if you can. I just get muddled and feel **really sleepy when she talks,**" Ellen the Elephant says to you, *and close your eyes, now.*

Muddled Mouse starts to talk: "I'm looking for sleep, thinking that it might be possible to let **a sleepy feeling like that grow** and make me even more sure that I can **see myself sleep,** and at the same time . . .

". . . the more I think about other things, it makes me, **now, even more tired,** so fuzzy, as if sleep has a feeling, and I can let that fuzzy feeling swirl around inside me, getting stronger and reminding me that . . .

". . . **it's time to sleep now,** so that means the things I'm thinking I'm not doing don't actually get done, so all my **focus now is on relaxing,** muddling, and so good when I think about how the story . . .

". . . is now making me think about what the story says and ignore everything else, and the more I think about anything except **sleeping now, the more sleepy I get,** if I could double that feeling, of complete relaxation and **heavy eyelids and** . . .

". . . *just close my eyes,* then it would **happen now,** then and right away too, as if sleep is **just something that happens,** *without any effort at all, and ever so easily sleep comes to you,* so when I try not to . . .

". . . **fall asleep,** that's exactly what I'm **going to do now,** sleep soundly all night, secure in the knowledge that I can feel completely safe and confident within myself and enjoy it my whole life. Aah . . ."

"Oh, how sleepy I am," Muddled Mouse says, and **falls asleep at once on her pillow** and sleeps soundly all night through [yawn].

The forest opens out, and up ahead you see the beach where you're going to sleep soundly all night. Together, Ellen the Elephant and you walk on slowly and feel a sleepy relaxation. It's very clear that you, **now are extremely tired** and are longing to fall asleep.

Daddy Elephant is waiting sleepily on the path to walk with you the last few steps to sleep, which is so close now. That makes you feel **even calmer and safer now,** *and you just relax, aah . . .*

As Ellen the Elephant's eyelids are closing, Daddy Elephant tells you very slowly about how he once fell asleep instantly while he was thinking lots of sleepy thoughts. "It's as if you fall asleep quicker and quicker each evening, when you now focus on sleep and on sleeping soundly [yawn]."

Daddy Elephant goes on and says, "When your body chooses to relax now, it's easy for you to fall fast asleep. Maybe you don't notice it yourself, now, that you're really tired and just want to fall asleep. Your body is telling you that it's time to just let your eyelids close, they're twice as heavy. I can see that you're so very tired and are going to sleep soundly all night through when you close your eyelids, now."

Much more relaxed, you keep walking slowly down, slowing down.

"Soon we'll be at the place where I fall fast asleep. I hope you'll want to fall asleep with me," Ellen says encouragingly in her very sleepiest voice.

"We're here at last," Ellen the Elephant says. **"I'm so sleepy,** I can't wait to lie down in my bed and **sleep deeply and soundly all night through."**

"For Ellen to be able to fall asleep, she needs your help," Daddy Elephant says. "You sleep best when you fall asleep too."

He explains, "If you're not already lying down, lie down now. You have to sleep for as long as you can, or at least pretend to so that Ellen the Elephant really believes that you're asleep and can also fall sound asleep. Start by pretending to be asleep, to help your friend Ellen, **fall asleep now."**

Daddy Elephant calmly tucks Ellen in. *"There . . . close your eyes again and relax. Do your very best to remember what you usually do when you fall asleep, and do the same thing now. If you do it for long enough, you and Ellen the Elephant will fall sound asleep too."*

Ellen the Elephant says thank you for spending time with her today, and you close your eyes to fall asleep, happy in the knowledge that you too are going to, fall asleep now. She whispers "goodnight" to you before you travel off to dreamland together.

Now that Ellen the Elephant is asleep, you can sleep soundly too, all night through [yawn].

Sleep well, wonderful child.

TIPS FROM THE AUTHOR

I'm often asked how parents should use my books to make bedtime a success. My answer is always to *observe* your child and then *adapt* the story. Here are some questions and answers that give examples of how to observe and adapt the story to every unique child, as well as questions about the books.

I hope these suggestions will help you make the most of my sleep-promoting books. I should emphasize that no one knows your child as well as you do. This can only be advice for you to bear in mind when you read the book.

My child doesn't like me adding her name in the story. It wakes her up.
I would advise not to say your child's name in a situation like that. Still, most children think it's fun that their name is included in the story. It makes them more connected with the message of the book.

Sometimes we read to more than one of our children at the same time. Should we say all the children's names where it says [name]?
Try it out. What happens? If they like it, keep doing it; otherwise, skip saying the children's names. It's perfectly OK to address the story to one unnamed child, though, because each child will absorb the story into his or her thoughts, so the story will speak specifically to that child.

My child thinks it sounds odd when I emphasize some words or read with a more soothing voice.
One solution is not to emphasize the words so heavily and to read a little more quickly if your child thinks it's going too slowly. You can also read the story normally to start with, without emphasis, or at a more even tempo, and still get your child to relax and feel tired. Try different approaches, and remember to have fun while you're doing so.

I've discovered that my child falls asleep more quickly at a particular part of the book, so I read the same section several times until my child falls asleep. Is that OK?
Absolutely – that's an excellent idea! You can also skip passages or pages if you notice that they somehow stimulate your child.

Do I have to finish the whole story even if my child has fallen asleep already on the second page?
Of course not, as long as you're sure your child really is fast asleep even when you leave the room. A lot of parents have told me that their children sleep more soundly throughout the night after they've listened to the story, so it can be a good idea to keep reading for a while after you think your child has fallen asleep because it might help him or her relax even more and reach a wonderful deep sleep.

The book is boring and doesn't stimulate my child's imagination.
My books are not intended to replace the wonderful picture books and chapter books you read with your child. My books are specifically for the time when your child needs to go to sleep, and therefore I don't want the book to be too exciting, as it will have the opposite effect and it will take longer for your child to fall asleep. Even so, I have tried to find a balance where the child's imagination is stimulated by inviting them to imagine things and by including a number of different characters in the books.

I've followed all the advice you've given me, but I still can't get my child to want to listen to the story.
It might be worth trying the audiobook instead, then you can snuggle up together. Or perhaps try one of the other books in the series. The books feature different characters and settings that might catch your child's interest long enough for him or her to want to listen to the story and be lulled to sleep. Reading the story is like rocking your child to sleep with words.

For what age are your sleep-promoting books recommended?
I have received letters saying that everyone from eight-month-old babies to adults with lifelong sleeping problems have managed to fall asleep to my bedtime stories. For that reason, they are not aimed at any specific age. But I do recommend testing and perhaps adapting the content of the story depending on the child's age. For adults, I usually recommend the audiobooks. A lot of people have said those have helped them fall asleep.

SUCCESS FACTORS

Here are some success factors based on what parents have told me after reading the first book in the series, *The Rabbit Who Wants to Fall Asleep*:

- Be persistent
- Create a habit
- Prepare before bedtime
- Focus on relaxation

Be Persistent
Even if your child doesn't fall asleep after you have read the whole story the first time, try reading it again. Give the book a real chance, even reading it through a couple of times. I remember a letter from one family in particular who said that bedtime could take up to five hours each evening. So they started to read *The Rabbit Who Wants to Fall Asleep*. The first evening, they read the whole story two and a half times before their child fell asleep. The following evening, they only needed to read the story once. Over the next few evenings, the length of time shrank further, and by the time they sent their letter, a week or so later, they were down to about eight minutes per evening. Bedtime went from five hours to just eight minutes, thanks to their persistence and faith in the book.

Create a Habit
Read the book several times over a period of time in order to create a habit, which will help your child feel secure enough to relax into the story and want to go to sleep. Parents have told me how *The Rabbit Who Wants to Fall Asleep* has become a natural part of their bedtime, that both child and parent know the book by heart, and that the child quickly falls asleep each evening. My wife and I had a similar experience with our son. We started playing him the audiobook while he was still in the womb, when we were going to sleep, so he made the mental connection between the story and sleep. After he was born, we played the audiobook every evening when it was time to go to sleep. Now, he is three years old and falls asleep easily in the evenings, with or without the audiobook, because he has learned to relax. Whenever he's sick or if we're travelling, we use the audiobook to help him feel safe and calm when it's time to go to bed.

Prepare Before Bedtime
In order to get the best results with the story, your child should be worn out before you read it. There are, however, examples where parents have said that their very active child has managed to fall asleep right at the start of the story. You can also prepare your child before you read the bedtime story by communicating in a special way. Here are a few examples of what you might say:

"You're starting to look tired, even if you might not be aware of it yet."

"It looks like your eyelids are getting heavier and heavier. It'll soon be time to go to sleep."

"You're getting sleepier and sleepier, aren't you [yawn]?"

"Tonight we're going to read a magical story that might make you want to fall asleep, maybe even before the story ends."

"You know that story we read in the evenings, the one that helps you fall asleep? It seems like you're falling asleep quicker and easier each time we read it. That must feel wonderful."

"Tonight I'm going to read a magical story that helps elephants, rabbits and lovely children like you fall asleep."

"You're only allowed to read this magical story when it's time to go to sleep because you're going to end up falling asleep every time we read it."

Focus on Relaxation

We are all different, of course, and have different strategies to process information. Some children will want to look at the pictures while you read the story, and some prefer just to listen. If your child is able to lie down in bed and listen to the story instead of looking at the pictures, there will be less visual information to process and your child will be more focused on what you're saying. Since the entire story is based on suggestions that you read on how to relax and fall asleep, it will make it easier to drift off to dreamland when you read and your child only has to focus on your voice. Lying in bed and just listening is all the more important for your child if you're reading from a tablet.

Good luck with my sleep-promoting books!

© ELIN CARLHOLT

ABOUT THE BOOK AND THE AUTHOR

Carl-Johan Forssén Ehrlin is a groundbreaking bestselling author whose first children's book, *The Rabbit Who Wants to Fall Asleep*, became a global phenomenon. It was the first self-published book to top Amazon's bestseller list. Thanks to satisfied parents telling their friends about the book and writing about it on social media, word about its magic spread. With more than a million copies sold around the world in just a few months, *The Rabbit Who Wants to Fall Asleep* quickly became an international success. Today the book has been translated into more than forty-three languages in forty-four countries.

The Little Elephant Who Wants to Fall Asleep is the second book in the series. All books in the series are intended to help children to relax and quickly fall asleep at bedtime.

Carl-Johan Forssén Ehrlin is a behavioural scientist with a bachelor's degree in psychology and teaches communications at a Swedish university. He is also a life coach and leadership trainer. Carl-Johan has combined all these skills and experiences in developing the techniques in this book. Read more about the author at carl-johan. com or on his Facebook pages: Carl-Johan Forssén Ehrlin and *The Rabbit Who Wants to Fall Asleep*.

ABOUT THE ILLUSTRATOR

Sydney Hanson was raised in Minnesota alongside numerous pets, and her illustrations and paintings still reflect a love for animals and the natural world. In addition to her book illustrations, Sydney is an experienced 2-D and 3-D production artist who has worked for several animation companies, including Nickelodeon and Disney Interactive. She lives in Los Angeles.

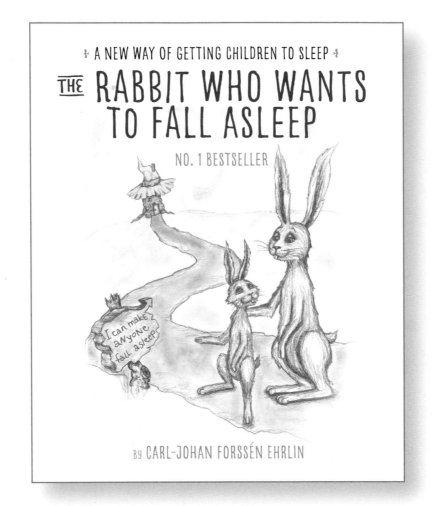